LUMIERE
The Reaper's Daughter

K.A. Hambly

Also by K.A.Hambly
The Town Halloween Forgot, The Curse of Willow Creek

A special thank you to Charlotte Kane for the cover design and
Alisha. A for the poem she contributed.

'You must see with eyes unclouded by hate. See the good in that which is evil, and the evil in that which is good. Pledge yourself to neither side, but vow instead to preserve the balance that exists between the two.'
Hayao Miyazaki

Hegira
By A Alisha.

We hid under the kitchen table
from the denizens of the pit
I slept on my side to avert the light
of the setting sun
In the corner of my eye,
I saw your luminescent smile
You pointed to the green canopy
Outside the window and said:
We belong there.
Disillusioned, we set ghosts on fire
You took my hand and tugged
as we hastened toward the glow
We ping-ponged between the trees,
between heaven and hell
- God knows we had the abrasions
to show for it -
The clearing was vast
The stars pierced my soul
You leaned in for a lushious kiss,
and said:
I know.
Solitude cuts deep,
but we'll always have

right here. Right now.

Chapter One

It was time. My initiation into the family's business was about to get its official seal, and I, Lumiere, would be able to roam freely from the land of the dead to the world of the living.

'Lumiere,' a sprightly voice came from the doorway. 'Five minutes.'

I nodded, staring at my reflection in the mirror.

'Sure. Five minutes.' I seethed, brushing my dark bangs.

I glanced over at the door as Kochak, one of my father's personal assistants, closed the door behind him. I turned attentively to my vanity, skilfully applying my red lipstick. Jinx, my faithful black cat jumped on my lap, knocking my hand sideways.

'Aw, Jinx, look what you made me do.'

Panicking, I grabbed a handful of tissues, trying to remove the red mark, only making the smudge worse.

'I look like I've just been bashed in the face.' I scowled, frightening him away. 'Right.' I stood up, took one last look at my reflection, tugged down the hem of my black dress and put on my black velvet initiation gloves. 'This is it, Jinx.' His big, blue eyes looked up at me from the window ledge. 'Wish me luck, eh?'

He hissed back, and I patted him on the head, blew out the candles and stepped into the hallway.

Candles lit the way, casting wavering shadows along the red carpet. I sucked in a breath and headed left to the ballroom. Normally this walk would take me less than two minutes, but tonight I was savouring every footstep and moment of freedom I had left. I turned right down another hall and then left again where there were two big black double doors. They had intricate designs of dragons my Father had commissioned from the old artist, Leonardo. There was a cry, and I looked down at my feet.

'Jinx, what are you doing here?' I whispered as I heard the door unlocking.

I turned to face the door, hands by my side.

The doors swung open into a place of opulence. Black marble paved the way illuminated by Gothic chandeliers to a black throne where my father was sitting, waiting for my arrival. Alongside the walls were figures in black, people who worked closely with my family. I hated being the centre of attention, especially as my heels were also tapping against the shiny floor.

'Jinx,' I whispered, turning back to see my faithful old cat following me.

'May I present to you my daughter, Lumiere.' My father, a tall man, dressed in black leather trousers and a three-quarter length black velvet coat, held out his arms to me as I approached. It was no fun being the daughter of the Reaper, but I suppose immortality had its advantages.

'Dad, why couldn't we have made this ceremony... a bit more private?' I whispered, leaning towards his ear.

His grey eyes settled on me, and he arched a dark brow.

'Lumiere,' he whispered back, 'this is your initiation ceremony into the family business. You don't think I will take this lightly, do you?' He smiled.

He wasn't the type of man to take anything lightly, so I should've known this whole debacle would be on a grand scale. On my sixteenth birthday he took me to Disneyland. The Hell version. I'll tell you about that another time.

I stepped up onto the stage, overlooking the sea of faces staring back up at me. My grandmother always told me that if you're nervous in public places to put on a pair of sunglasses. So that's what I was about to do, except I had forgotten them. I snapped my fingers, and in the palm of my hand was a new pair of *Ray Bans*.

'Lumiere, your attention please.' Father asked.

I glared at him and slipped the glasses on. He picked up a sword from a small round table beside his throne and walked over to me waiting nervously.

'Eighteen years ago on this very day, darkness was expelled from this place for a few moments when my darling wife gave birth to our precious daughter, Lumiere.'

Oh please Dad, just get on with it. I rolled my eyes; sure the entire audience's eyes were on me.

'And now, eighteen years later, she has grown into a smart young lady, who will work alongside me. I now initiate her into the Reaper's Souls.'

He lowered the sword across my shoulders to cheers and applause.

I tried to force a smile, but if I am honest, this was not the career I would've chosen for myself. They say life is what you make it, but my life was hell. I mean that literally by the way. I waved at them and this was followed by another rapturous applause.

At the after-party, I stood awkwardly by a bowl of punch, sipping on my fourth glass when father, or as he was known to people, Mr. Reaper, came by with another man in tow. He was built like a wrestler, with an embarrassing eighties mullet. I hoped he was not going to try to set me up on another date.

'Lumiere, I'd like you to meet, Marshall.'

Ugh. Trying to stay polite, I held out my hand when he grabbed it and smothered it in his saliva.

'Yeah, nice to meet you too.' I yanked my hand away but he pulled it back and dragged me onto the dance floor.

'Like dancing, do you?' I smiled as my feet were barely reaching the floor.

'Yes, but only with pretty ladies.' He said, flashing his rotten teeth.

I winced and released myself from his grip.

'Ladies room,' I shrugged, meandering my way through the crowd of people.

Out in the hallway, I saw my father having a hushed conversation with Strax, the gatekeeper to our underworld. Dad patted him on the shoulder and left, but Strax sensed me and flicked his green eyes towards me. Man, he gave me the shivers. Even my father being what he is, Strax, with his stick frame, and wisp of white hair on his bony head had me wanting to run for cover.

Not wanting to hang about, I headed straight for my room. There was no way I was going back to that party to be set up with more Neanderthals.

I unlocked my door when I felt a hand on my shoulder.

'Going somewhere?' I turned around.

Strax.

'And what do you want?' I asked, forgetting how quick he was on his feet.

'Your father asked me to give you this.'

He held out his hands. In the palm was a small black velvet bag. 'He wants you to go out tonight to collect a soul.'

'Tonight?' I gasped. 'Are you kidding me? This is my initiation ceremony.'

I thought I'd play on the fact that this was *my* night, and nothing was meant to spoil it. I did not want to catch souls. My dream was to be, well, just a normal person with a normal job like I had seen on Earth television.

He looked scornfully at me with his bulging green eyes. It was freaking me out. I guess that was it then. It didn't look as though I had any say in the matter.

Chapter Two

Allow me to tell you something about Hell. I have often heard humans say their lives are Hell and I look at them and think, 'Human, you have no idea what Hell is until you have been here.' At the time I didn't realise it was used to express how crap their lives were, but honestly, Hell is no fun. Not for me, at least. I wanted more than it had to offer.

When souls are condemned to eternal damnation they are sent to a small box room. It's like a Hell version of a sauna, except it's very, very hot. A human would not endure the intensity of the heat. They would just combust before they entered. Luckily, or maybe, not so luckily, depends on your views, when a soul is brought to Hell by a Reaper's Soul, their earthly bodies are left in the Earth plane, for their relatives to grieve over. You get my drift, right? Well, a soul is much tougher than the body that encased it. Souls are eternal and never, ever die. If you're good, you'll go to my Uncle's place called Heaven, but we call it 'The Other Room.' If you're very, very bad on the Earth plane, we pick you up, and you will sweat out your evil deeds in the Sauna. Or the Poker Room as it's also known. Anyway, I was soon to be a Reaper's Soul, but honestly, it's the most boring job, ever.

Well, it didn't seem like I had a choice in the matter just yet. I set my bag down on my dressing table and walked over to my wardrobe. If I was going out tonight, I wanted to look good. Clothes were my passion. If it was black, red or purple, I'd wear it. As I flicked through the pile of black clothes the bedroom door knocked lightly.

'Yeah, what do you want?' I shouted thinking it was Strax or my father.

'Lumiere, it's your mother.'

I glanced over my shoulder. 'Oh, hi, Mum.'

Mum was a tall, curvy woman with long wavy, black hair. Her face was as pale as the moonlight, and her eyes, like mine were light blue.

'All prepared?' she asks.

Her voice was like silk. When she used to read me stories as a child, it always lulled me to sleep in no time.

I turned my attention back to the drama of finding a decent outfit.

'Not yet.' I held up a black and purple corset. 'What do you think?'

'Hmm, yes, it suits you. But don't you think you should wear something a little more, practical, maybe?' She smiled. 'You could be climbing in windows, or running from snarling dogs...' She paused, and thoughtfully gazed out of the window. 'I wouldn't say the dogs so much, our Hell hounds are far worse, but, you never know, Lumi.'

'Yeah, you're probably right, as usual. So how about these leather trousers and my *69 Eyes* T. Shirt?'

'Perfect.'

'Great.'

I started to undress, and I still had no idea why Mum had come into my room. She seemed concerned.

'So why does Dad want me to go out tonight? Talk about throwing me in at the deep end.'

I removed my top, putting on the corset. Mum helped tie it up.

'That's what your father is like, unfortunately. We got engaged two days after meeting.'

'Seriously?' I asked, looking at her smiling from the mirror.

'Yes. He's the type of man that knows what he wants and isn't afraid to go out and get it.'

I threw on my T. shirt, listening intently to her talking. Until now, I had never heard about my parent's first meeting.

'We met at a vampire convention in London.'

'The Earth London?' I asked, intrigued.

'There's only one true London, Lumi, but yes. I was a mortal at the time working a nine to five day in a clothes shop to keep my head above water.'

'Jeez, Mum, I never realised.'

'No, nobody would think it now looking at me, but it's true.'

'So tell me about London and the vampires?'

'Since my teens I had been fascinated with vampires, you know, hanging around graveyards and clubs. So when a friend asked if I wanted to go along with them to a vampire convention, I just jumped at the chance. I was twenty-one at the time.'

'Were they real vampires? I know we have a few of those here.'

She laughed.

'No. Nothing like the ones we have here. These were humans pretending to be vampires, but still, it was fascinating.'

'And Dad? Was he dressed as a vampire?'

She turned to look at me.

'Your father was with Vlad at the time. They are great friends, you know. I suppose it's cliché to say, but our eyes met across the room and it was love at first sight.'

'So if you're human, Mum, how are you immortal now?'

'Ah, that Lumi is a very delicate matter,' she sighed.

I sat down on the bed.

'Oh come on, you can't leave out the rest now.'

'Okay. Scoot up then.'

She lay down next to me, and we both gazed up at the sky. We didn't have ceilings, or roofs. From here we could look up at the stars.

'Our first meeting was intense, and it still is. When I saw him, he came over and introduced himself to me as Luc. He sounded French. His dark eyes drew me in, and when he touched my hand and brought it to his lips, I knew it was love and I'd do anything for him.'

'And did you?'

'Of course. I gave him my soul. We arranged for Vlad to make me immortal that evening. I never returned home and my parents never knew what happened to me. I feel sad about that.'

Now I understood the sadness I'd sometimes see in my mother's eyes. She'd been a human. . This was truly amazing. I now understood where my feelings came from about the Earth plane. I was one of them.

'Do you ever wished you could go back?'

'What purpose would that serve? I'm happy here, Lumi. Hell is my home.'

Chapter Three

After hearing Mum's revelation, I wasn't sure I could ever look at her in the same way again. I was buzzing with this new information regarding my heritage. It made my job a little easier tonight knowing that I had a connection to mortals.

'Mum, I best go and find Dad. Was there anything else bothering you?'

'No, Lumi, nothing else. If you want me later, I'll be in my library.' She kissed my forehead and held my hands. 'Be careful tonight, okay. Your father has been sent another threatening letter.'

'Another? Has he any idea who is sending them?' I asked, flabbergasted she didn't mention this earlier.

'No I don't think so unless he isn't telling me something. When you get back, let me know, okay? I know you're an adult now, but I worry about you.' She wrapped her arms around me tightly and then cupped my face. 'Love you, baby doll.' She said, unable to let her tears fall, and left the room.

What a night, eh? I was exhausted already and my job hadn't even begun.

I grabbed the velvet bag from the vanity and closed the door behind me. I expected father to be waiting at the Shute for me. The Shute is where we get sent to our destination points to collect souls.

What my father doesn't know is I have been using it secretly for years. My only ambition in my immortal life was to live on the Earth plane. I've always felt connected to the place and now I know why.

Walking down yet another corridor to the Shute, I saw Lucinda, my little sister playing with her Skull and Bones board game on the floor.

'Hey, there's no fun in playing on your own.' I said.

She looked up at me with her big blue eyes. 'But I am not alone.'

Yeah, that'd be right. My sister had inherited our mother's gift of seeing the soul long after we'd take it.

'Are you going soul gathering?' she asks as I knelt down beside her watching the skull move across the board of its own accord.

'Yeah, Dad wants me to collect one tonight. I don't see what the rush is.'

Lucinda smirked and went back to her game. I got up and carried on walking down the hall.

'Lumiere, come on girl, what has taken you so long?' My father huffed, standing outside the door, hands on his hips.

'Dad, calm down.' I groaned.

He turned around, pushed the door open, setting off the lights. Yes, we have artificial lights. According to my dad he practically gave Edison the idea. They were at a party together where Dad just happened to be collecting a soul that evening. Over a game of chess the topic of conversation turned into how gloomy it was to live on Earth without means of light except for the use of candles. Dad remarked it was like living in Hell, to which Edison agreed. Dad supposedly laughed at him, saying he had no freaking idea what it was like to live in Hell and would he like to come and see. This had Edison in fits of laughter, and Dad, drunk as usual, told him about his idea to create artificial light. Imagine that, the Lord of Hell and darkness himself, giving mortals the recipe for light. Yes, he was an idiot at times.

'Damn,' he cussed, covering his eyes. 'I always forget how bright these blasted bulbs are.'

I laughed. 'Sure you're not a vampire?'

'Unfortunately not. Your uncle scored with that. Anyway, Lumi,' he said, pointing towards a metal arch that took up most of the room. 'This is the gateway to Earth.'

Like I didn't know. Oh and by the way, Dad had two brothers. I'll get to the one in The Other Room soon as he was practically an outcast. But just to clarify, their parents created the universe and there are three planes of existence, and my uncle, the vampire was given the void to look after. It's where we give mortals the chance to decide if they have any more business to finish on the Earth plane before we make the final decision where to allocate them.

'Okay,' I said, walking towards it. 'What's my job for tonight then and why can't you go?' I asked.

He folded his arms defensively and stood tapping his pointy boots on the floor.

'Lumi, when I ask you to do something, I don't expect to be questioned. Now, all I want you to do is go to New York, pick up a soul, and fetch it back. In fact, I am going to send Ulrich with you.'

Oh great. Ulrich was Dad's little snitch. A half troll, half goblin.

'Why? Don't you trust me?'

'It's not about trust, Lumi. This is a very big case. I need to be certain it doesn't go awry.'

He poured himself a drink, something he did not do often. I didn't know if I ought to press it any further, and so slumped down on the black swivel chair beside the desk. Official looking papers were strewn all over.

'What is really going on, Dad?' I asked, sifting through the hundreds of documents. There was a clink of glass. 'Dad?' I asked, watching him pour another drink.

He cleared his throat, swallowed another glass of whiskey, and took a deep breath.

'Well?'

'I owe money to a few influential people on earth.' He said, casually.

'By influential, I take it you mean underground crime lords?'

I sat back, crossing my arms, amazed he got himself involved with them in the first place.

'Yes, Lumi.' He shrugged. 'I needed the money to pay your uncle for his share of the family business.'

'But, Dad, you're the reaper, why do you need to borrow money from humans?' He looked shifty and avoided eye contact. 'You lost it all, didn't you? Gambling.'

'Well, Lumi, a man has to have some vices, you know. Even the devil himself.' He laughed.

The door opened, and the atmosphere in the room shifted to a dank and depressing state, not that it needed much help. I lowered my level of vision to the bottom half of the door and in walked, Ulrich. He had backcombed, big, red eighties hair, and a face that would not melt a thousand hearts if he spent the rest of eternity trying. He'd most likely break them and according my sources he already had.

'I got your message, Sir.' He strolled over to my father, acknowledging my presence with a flick of his dark, beady eyes. I guess the feeling was mutual then.

'Ulrich, you know what's what regarding this mission tonight, just make sure my daughter does exactly what she is meant to do, and nothing else.' He turned to face me. 'Nothing else, Lumi. Don't pull any fast ones and go off on some jaunt around New York on your own.'

Why does he have to go on repeating himself? 'Okay, Dad. Now whom am I meant to collect?'

I took a black leather notepad from my pocket and a pen from Dad's pot on his desk.

'Daniel Lee. He's supposed to be involved in a traffic accident tonight by Central Park.'

'Description?'

There was no answer. I looked up from my notepad at Dad, standing there with a raised brow.

'Lumi, you will know when you see him.'

It was not the response I was looking for and the look I gave him left him in no doubt about that.

'Oh, okay. He's about five foot nine, slim build with dark brown hair.'

'How do you know him then?' I asked, flipping the notebook closed, and stuffing it in my leather trouser pocket.

'Never you mind, Lumi. Now, go with Ulrich. When you arrive in New York, you will have about an hour to wait. And, please, *wait.*' He said, dragging out the last word like he didn't completely trust me to do the job.

'Yes, Dad.' I mockingly saluted to him.

Ulrich smirked, and I raised my fist at him.

'Can you two please get on for once?' Dad said, pouring himself another drink.

'So, ready when you are.' I gestured towards the gate.

'No when you are.' Ulrich laughed waiting for me to go first.

I clenched my fist into a ball, and was about to throw a punch, when Dad intervened.

'Just get the hell out of here.' He yelled, blowing a bulb.

'A bit difficult isn't it when we're already in Hell.' I laughed.

He pointed a finger at me, and I knew it was time to quit the witty remarks I am so well known for.

'Okay, Ulrich. Let's go.' I said, stepping into the gate.

Ulrich typed in the destination on the keypad, and there was a mechanical whirring sound that emanated from the metal above my head.

'And we're ready.' Ulrich said, quickly stepping into the gate.

I felt like pushing him out, but that would only piss Dad off even more.

A flash of white light surrounded me and I closed my eyes. When I felt the chilly air against my face I opened my eyes to find I was sitting down on a busy sidewalk. I almost got trampled on by a woman in a pair of *Jimmy Choo's*. I hoped it was New York as I've never been here before. I took stock of my bearings. It was New York alright; anyone would recognise the Statue of Liberty across the water... Statue of Liberty? I gasped and got to my feet. Shit. I was in the wrong place, but how?

'Ulrich?' I looked down and Ulrich wasn't there. 'Oh no. Now what has happened?' I was about a mile from where I should be.

I turned around, smacking my face into a passing pedestrian.

'Are you alright, Miss?' A young, English man asked.

'Yeah, I think so.' I rubbed my forehead grateful he wasn't a lamppost.

Brushing away my bangs, I looked up to see the most stunning, sparkly, brown eyes looking back at me.

'Hi,' he said, smiling.

'Hi,' I replied, excited to be speaking to a human. A hot one at that.

'Are you lost?' He asked.

'Um.' I didn't know if I was, or if I was meant to be here. 'No, not really, but thanks for asking. You know, I may be a little confused, you see. Have you seen a little guy, looks like an imp; ugly. May have stepped out of the 80's?'

He laughed. No. I haven't.'

I'm sure he thought I was trying to chat him up, but it was a genuine, honest question. But then I realised. I'm on Earth. People don't have creepy, little fuckers for companions. And then I saw his dog.

'Oh, what a cute dog.' I bent down, patting this great husky dog on his head.

Lumi, what are you doing?

'His name his Thor.'

'Oh Thor. I know him...'

As the words left my mouth I realised how crazy that sentence would sound had I finished it. So I shut up. I was sounding like a demented moron that has escaped from a padded cell. I got to my feet, cleared my throat and apologised.

'Sorry, I must sound like an idiot. Anyway, sorry to bother you, I'm just off to the park, you know, for a walk.'

I hadn't spoken to many humans before so my mouth had the tendency to run away with me at times.

'You sound pretty cool.' He smiled. 'If you're not busy do you mind us tagging along with you? We're off to the park for a walk. My name is Dan by the way. Yours?'

Oh shit, what have I gone and done? 'Sure. It's Lumiere.' The words escaped my mouth before I had time to think.

Oh well, I had about an hour like Dad said. The crossing wasn't far. I was sure I could make it to my destination in that time.

Chapter Four

It didn't happen. Half an hour had passed, and I was still sat talking to Dan. He had me wrapped in his knowledge of Art and the Renaissance period. Being an immortal meant I had copious amounts of time to study and learn. So suffice to say I knew a lot more than him, but it was nice to sit and talk to someone for a change.

I checked my watch.

'Do you have to be somewhere?' He asked.

'Sort of.' But before I could say anything else, I saw his eyes light up with excitement.

'I'm going to the university's ball tonight would you care to join me?'

My face must've disappointed him.

'Oh, I'm sorry. I thought, by the way you were dressed you were going to the Halloween party. Sorry, I shouldn't make assumptions like that.'

'No, no offence taken. This is how I look every day. So, what is the university's party in aid of then?' I asked, like a dumbass. How could I, the daughter of the reaper forget our most important day of the year?

'It's Halloween tonight. I'm just going drop Thor off at home and make my way there.'

'Ah, no. I'm not I'm afraid, but if I could make it, I would've loved to have gone with you.'

He looked disappointed, and I was intrigued enough to go and see how the humans celebrated my favourite day of the year.

'Okay, I'll come for a bit.' I said, checking my father's pocket watch again. 'If you don't mind, I'll catch up with you tonight? I have something I must do first.'

'Yes, I'd love that. I'll meet you outside the main block at nine?'

'Nine it is then.'

I made a mental note that I had to stop agreeing to things I wasn't sure of, but Daniel was a good enough reason to attend this party. But before I could do that, I had to do what I actually came for; to take this soul to Hell. Usually, Dad would send them to Limbo where his brother Patrick would talk to them, sometimes for days on ends. As he was a vampire, time as *we* know it made no difference to him, but to the poor souls who would arrive there, a day may feel like a millennium. It was a sufficient amount of time for them to ascertain where they should end up in the afterlife. I had known my uncle agreeing to send souls back to the Earth plane whereby they would re-learn the lessons again, so that they would, when the time was right again, arrive back in Limbo and they would go directly where they were supposed to go. Some never learned though.

It got dark. I had about twenty minutes before this event was supposed to happen and I know if I didn't do what Dad had asked there would be more than Hell to pay on the menu tonight.

I arrived at my destination, on time. I maybe had a minute to spare. I looked nervously at the traffic lights, and then at the crowd of people waiting to cross. One of those poor buggers would meet my dad tonight. As much as I loved him, he wasn't to be reckoned with when he was angry, and I got the sense that whoever it was I had to take was connected to his business affairs.

I took the bag from my pocket and waited. As crazy as it sounds I rather wished Ulrich would have been here. I still had no idea where he went.

'Here goes.' The cars came to a halt, and the yellow sign flashed. I opened the bag and waited staring at the sea of faces approaching me. They were a mixture of old and young, some relatively young. I had my eye on a stocky man in a navy business suit, but that would be so cliché if it was him. Why did he have to dress like a business man, he could...

'Daniel?' What was he doing here? As the crowd brushed past me, I could see him at the back, and then, to my horror, a motorcycle came roaring down the street, lost control and skidded along the tarmac. The cyclist came off, and the bike was still trailing down the road. I pushed my way through the crowd that were now going crazy, screaming for him to move, but there was no chance. He turned to look in my direction. I screamed, flailing my arms like a mad woman for him to get out of the way, but it was fruitless. As he faced the on-coming bike, it smacked into him, sending him into mid-air like a rag doll.

'Noooo!' I cried, falling to my knees, hands covering my face.

'Lumiere.' I heard a voice.

I looked to my left. In the bustle of people, I saw Kochak who was also a Reaper's Soul. He stood next to the cyclist who had just been killed. The man looked as though there was nothing wrong with him, except he was dead.

'What?' I spat, angrily.

'You're meant to collect the soul.' He pointed.

Reluctantly I turned to the right. An ambulance had turned up now, and there were people gathered around his body on the floor. My gaze turned slightly to the right again, next to the ambulance and there he was, standing scared stiff looking down at them trying to save his body.

I stuffed the bag in my jacket pocket as there was no way I could use it on him. No, I was going to take him back my way. I walked over to him standing alone looking petrified. I had never lost a friend before so to say I understood death was a lie.

'Daniel.' I whispered, slipping my hand his.

He turned his head slightly to look at me. Tears streamed down his face. Once a soul had leaped from its body everything they see on Earth happens at a much faster pace.

'What's happened to me, Lumiere?' His lips quivered.

There was no way to put this lightly.

'You're dead.'

'I was crossing the road just moments ago. How?' He seemed to have registered something and looked me in the eyes. 'How can you see me?'

I wasn't trained enough for this. Damn my bloody father. This man did not deserve to go to Hell. He didn't have a bad aura.

'I've come to take you.' I said softly.

'Take me? What are you, Lumiere?

'I'm sort of like an angel, except I take souls to the Underworld.'

I felt ashamed of what I was, and couldn't look him in the eyes.

'I'm going to Hell? Really? What did I do to deserve this?' He shook.

'I don't know, but I'm sure it has been a mix up on my Dad's part.' I hoped.

'I never thought it would be like this. I thought angels were meant to be dressed in white, and there would be a heaven.'

He looked up at the sky.

'There is a heaven, but look, we must leave before I get into trouble.'

'I can't.' He refused. 'I have too much I wanted to do.'

'I'm really sorry, but this was your time.' I shrugged.

I didn't know what else I could do or say to make him feel better. I mean, could you make souls feel better about their death and the fact they are summoned to Hell? No, I don't think so.

It took a few minutes to calm him. When I finally got him to agree to come with me, I turned to see Kochak tapping his watch, hinting for me to hurry this along.

'Hold my hand.' I said, smiling at him. 'This won't hurt, I promise. I'll take care of you.' But he pulled away from me, and his soul began to fade. I turned to Kochak. 'What's happening?' I could see the panic in his eyes.

'He's going back into his body.' He gasped. 'Come on, Lumi, best we go home. Your father is going to be pissed to say the least.'

Chapter Five

I was home. I hadn't spoken to my father yet, but I heard he was very angry. I mean, why would he take somebody as sweet as Daniel? I gazed out of my bedroom window down on the bloody furnaces below. It was just too damned hot here and I craved the Earth for its seasons.

'Dinner is ready, Lumiere. Your mother has requested you in the ballroom.' Kochak said, rather softly.

It was unusual for him to be so kind. Whatever is going on now?

I grabbed Jinx and set off for dinner. I was starved to be honest with you. The last I ate was at the party last night, and even that seemed a million years ago right now.

As I entered the ballroom, Mum, who was sat at the very end of a long table, looked up, and smiled, gesturing to a seat next to her. I was a bit nervous as to why my father wasn't here. He would always lunch with us.

'Where's Dad?' I asked, taking my seat.

She put down her knife and fork and reclined back in her seat. 'He's not too happy about last night, Lumi.'

'Mum, it wasn't my fault. I had the soul, but he, for some very strange reason, went back into his body. I don't think that was meant to happen, but it did.'

'Calm down, Lumi. Did I say I blame you? No. And neither does your father.'

'Then what happened?' I asked.

'Your father's brother arranged for the soul to go back to its body. He's punishing your father for borrowing the money and getting himself into strife with the Earth crime lords.'

'So what has Daniel got to do with this?'

'Daniel?' She asked, curiously.

'He was the soul I was meant to collect. We got to talking before he had the accident.'

I looked down at my empty plate, biting my lip. I was waiting for some kind of lecture but it never came.

'That's a rather strange twist of events.'

'You think?' I looked up, thoughtfully.

'Usually we are not meant to engage with the souls we take before they die.'

'Well, then it is strange. He was nice though mum.'

'I can tell you're a bit smitten, Lumi, but it is not a wise idea. He's a human again now. For the time being at least.'

'Wait, you didn't tell me why Dad wanted to take him?'

'He's the son of one of the crime lords that is threatening your father. Unfortunately because of your father's gambling problems he has lost all the money he borrowed from your uncle. The crime lords know of your father's position, I guess you could say, and want to expose him.'

'So Dad took his son as bait?'

'Yes, but your uncle wants to teach him a lesson. You know those two never got on, even as children.'

'Now I see.'

'Yes. So, your father does not blame you. Now eat some food. We have the Halloween celebrations later.'

Halloween. How could I bloody forget again? And I promised Daniel I'd meet him at the university.

After lunch, I felt exhausted and wanted to be left alone for a while, so I headed to the library. The library is my favourite place in our entire house.

I remembered I had told Daniel that I had a thing for Gothic literature, which I do and I guess I wanted to impress him with a first edition copy of something or another.

The library housed every book that had ever been written on the Earth plane. It was cylinder in shape and vast with more books being added each day. Often times we would get advance copies of novels before they had ever been written. Those were the fun ones. I sat with the first edition of Dracula when I heard my sister singing, interrupting me.

'What are you reading?' She asked.

I looked up at her. She was wearing her long white nightie.

'Dracula. And what are you doing in here? You don't like books.'

'I know what you're planning to do.' She said, studying the cover of the book as though it would give her some clues.

'Okay, little snitch, what do you know?'

'You want to go to Earth tonight to meet that boy.'

'Okay, what are you after, Lucinda?'

'Nothing.'

'Seriously? You won't tell?'

'Nope. Not if you take me with you.'

I threw the book down on the table. 'You little brat. I can't do that; Mum would go crazy if she knew.'

She crossed her arms defiantly.

'Well, I may just tell her then.'

'Lucinda. I can't take you to Earth unless... you dress up as something for Halloween.' Ooh why did I have to go and say that?

'Thanks, Lumi. I'll behave I promise.' She ran out the door excitedly.

Crap. I am such an idiot at times.

I stuffed the Dracula book under my arm and left to go to my room to get ready.

The plan was to sneak out during the celebrations. My family invited everyone from Hell, so you can imagine the amount of people that would be here, not to mention, demons and whatnot.

Halloween is the most celebrated day here, so there were lots of people doing various jobs around the house. I wouldn't say it needed much in the way of decorations as we had them up all year long. But my father had some very special pieces that would only see the light of day once a year, well you get my drift. We're in Hell, it is forever dark here. I strolled through the living room, which is just another ballroom just in time to see Strax set up the replica of the original Addams family set.

'Hey.' He waved as I passed.

'Hey.' I said back, not in the mood to stop to chat or help.

'It's been a busy night, hasn't it?' He sniggered.

He obviously knew about the little muck-up with the soul. I wasn't going to give him the pleasure to gloat, so I ignored, and headed for the door to the staircase.

'Lumi. Just the girl I wanted to see.'

Oh, hi Dad,' I turned on my heel to face him.

He stood wearing an Alice Cooper T. shirt and black jeans that were ripped at the knee. He was forever in his heavy metal phase. I remembered the time he went to Donnington, you know, the music festival, and he got to hang out with all these rock stars. During another of his drunken binges he almost ended up summoning everyone back to Hell. Imagine that. Although, I think Ozzy would've been floored.

'What is it, Dad?'

'I heard it was a rough night?'

'Yeah, it wasn't the best.'

'I'm sorry, Lumi. I didn't know this would happen.'

'No, of course not. Well, look, never mind. I'm home now so no big deal, eh?'

'Come and sit with me for a bit.'

He gestured to the room next to the ballroom. It was his collectibles room. Dad was a big fan of Earth films and TV shows. Normally we would never be allowed in here. It was strictly off limits . He said there's at least a few thousands of pounds' in Earth money worth of stuff in here and if we'd break anything he would send us to the Chamber. So we never went in.

I sat down on his precious Star Trek chair, careful to keep my hands away from anything breakable.

'What's bothering you, Dad?'

He swept his hair back and then folded his arms.

'You obviously know about my debts? And trust me, Lumi, I am getting help for my gambling. It's just that I went off the rails a bit and ended up getting into serious trouble.'

'I know. Those men are planning to expose you.'

'Yes, yes they are. And your uncle isn't helping.' He seethed.

He relaxed a bit now and clasped his hands together, leaning in close as though he was about to reveal something.

'I'm going to expose myself to the world.'

'Oh, Dad.' I said, disgusted, recoiling back against the chair.

'No, Lumi, I didn't mean it that way. I meant; I want to tell the world I really exist.'

'Do you think it's a good idea, Dad?'

'Why not?' He exclaimed, throwing his hands up in the air.

'Well, the world is pretty messed up. I don't think it could handle you on top of everything else.'

'You think?'

'I know, Dad. Don't you watch Earth television shows? The people are already crazy.' I lied. 'There are wars, people arguing over religion.' I went on and on but he still seemed pretty adamant that it was a good idea.

'I do see your point, but I figured if I did it myself, it would be less dramatic than someone waltzing into a room and saying, 'Hell exists. Come and get your tickets for the theme park.' I tell you, Lumi that's what will happen next.' He said, wagging a finger.

'Ooh, give over, Dad.' Dad was a worrier despite his hard appearance.

'Well, I'd better think of something before I lose everything I have.'

'Dad, you're fretting over nothing.' I patted his arm. 'Look, I have to go and get ready for this party.'

He nodded. 'Okay. I am sorry, Lumi.'

Chapter Six

If Dad were to expose himself to the world, I cannot imagine what would happen. There is a possibility that they would think he was a lunatic, but there's something you ought to know about dad. He had supernatural powers that would blow your mind. Apart from telepathy, which was a natural trait of his, he could harness the power of any demon that would come within a metre of him. So, yes, dad was invincible. Unfortunately, he didn't possess the qualities to stop this gambling business.

So, today is Halloween. I left dad to go and get changed. Every year, Mum would buy me a new dress, black being the obvious colour, but the cut and style would be different. I haven't seen the dress yet. She kept it a secret.

I passed the kitchen on the way to my room. Hell is hot enough, so imagine the kitchens - they're worse. If it wasn't for the strict rules and regulations which dad adhered to, despite his rebellious nature I truly believe, the chefs would be quite happy to roam about in their underpants.

'Hi Louis.' I poked my head around the door.

'Hello, Madame Lumiere.'

Louis was our French waiter. He was tall, short sleeked black hair, and had an orange tan. He wasn't human though, he was a demon. You only had to look at the top of his head to see two red horns.

'What's cooking?'

'It's your favourite, pumpkin soup.' He gestured to the hot pans on the stove.

'You're awesome, Louey. I'll have some later.'

'Of course. See you later, Madame.'

It was high time I got ready. It wasn't until I saw Lucinda in the playroom that I remembered my promise.

'I've got my costume, Lumi. I promise it will be discreet.'

'Okay, squirt. You'd better not blow this for me or I'll make sure you'll pay me back for centuries to come. You wouldn't want that now, would you?'

She shook her head.

'No. So what's this boy like then?'

'Why are you so interested in this boy, huh? You were mysterious when I set off to collect his soul.'

She shrugged. I knew by her devious little smile something was up, but I didn't have time to get it out of her.

'Just promise you'll behave.'

'Pinky promise.'

Yeah, right. She was going to cause me bother, but I had dad to think of too. What if he was going to expose his identity to the world? My life was never easy.

I strolled into my room. My mum had already laid my dress out on my bed. It was a sleek, strapless, black dress that I fancied a while ago after seeing it in a magazine. So, it was now time for a shower.

Nothing like a shower to freshen up. So where was I? Oh yes, I'm about to attend our Halloween party, but only for a while. I plan to go back to Earth. It's such a fascinating place. All I've learned from humans so far has been from the television or books. It's not the same if you ask me. Which is why I wanted to meet Daniel.

'Are you coming, Lumi?' Mum yelled.

'I'll meet you down there.' I yelled back.

You're probably wondering if we ever sleep? Truth is, we don't need it much. I usually use it as an excuse to get away from the family, or if I need time by myself. I'm pretty sure mortals do that too, but I doubt they would admit it.

I refreshed my make-up and made my way to the party. I figured if I showed my face for a while they wouldn't end up missing me much when I left. I only reached the top of the staircase when I heard dad singing on the karaoke. Or should that have been screaming?

As I made my way down the stairs a centaur passed me. He smiled and then went about his business. The house was heaving with people. The only good thing about Halloween in Hell is that nobody has to buy a costume, they just came as themselves. Then, I spied The Three Sisters as they are known, huddled by a cauldron, sipping from tall flute glasses. They had long black hair and wore black dresses and capes.

The Three Sisters, who are witches if you hadn't already guessed, called out to me. They give me the shivers if I'm honest. They have the power to see into the future, something I had never been keen on after they called dad up one day to tell him the winning lottery numbers on the Earth plane. He ended up winning four million pounds, but Mum went crazy with him and told him to give the ticket away to somebody who needed it. For weeks later he went around sulking like a kid. Believe me, that is Hell.

'Lumiere,' Sasha, one of the witches cooed. 'We're sorry we missed your Initiation ceremony. We were away at Glastonbury that weekend spell casting.'

Like I cared

'Oh, you didn't miss much. Hope you enjoy the party.'

I was about to merge with the rest of the crowd and disappear but she grabbed my arm, pulling me close.

'Be very careful, Lumi about your choices. Everything has a cause an effect, and immortals are no exception to the rule.'

'Um, thank you. I'll remember that.' I said, edging away slightly. 'I've got to see Mum about something.'

I felt nervous. Whatever could they mean? Surely they didn't know about my plan?

I grabbed a glass of punch from a table as I made my way to the stage. Yes, we had a real stage. Dad was rocking with dead members of rock bands from the Earth plane. I'm pretty certain the guy in all leather was Elvis Presley.

I waved to dad who waved back rather enthusiastically. The music quietened down and dad took the microphone from Elvis. Oh please, no more singing.

'This next song is for my kids.' He said.

Everyone turned to look at me and my face went hot with embarrassment. I looked around for Lucinda, but she was nowhere to be seen. Did Dad know something I didn't?

The intro to *Aerosmith's I Don't Want To Miss A Thing* came on, and I felt an arm snake around my waist.

'Lovely to see you again.' The voice said.

I glanced up and smiled.

'Uncle Patrick? What are you doing here?'

Uncle Patrick was a lot like dad when it came to looks. He had short blood-red hair, a pale complexion with sharp green eyes and chiselled cheekbones.

'I just thought I'd stop by and see how my family are doing. Why? What's wrong?' He asked, sensing something was wrong.

'Oh, nothing.' I shrugged. 'It's just dad's in a bit of bother with Uncle David.'

He rolled his eyes. 'Let me guess. It's over money?'

'Yep.'

' Did you know Uncle David loaned him money?'

'No, Lumi, but I did wonder why he wouldn't come here tonight. I'll try to sort it, don't worry.' He smiled, flashing his pointed fangs.

Uncle Patrick had all the women lusting over him. It's probably why he wasn't given the job to take souls to eternal damnation because they'd all want to go with him. Hell is brimming over as it is and if this place got taken over by someone else, let me tell you, it would end in disaster.

'I'll speak to you later, Lumi.' He winked.

Time was getting on, and I promised to meet Daniel at nine o'clock Earth time. I checked my watch. It was eight thirty now, and I had to wade through a crowd of Uncle Fester lookalikes.

'Excuse me,' I said to one. 'Oh, please excuse me.' I said to the other.

I made it into the corridor wondering where the hell Lucinda had got to. She could be a horrible little brat at times but this was my only chance of escape. If I didn't leave now, while it was quiet, I'd never make it. Discreetly, I opened the door to the Shute, and closed it quietly behind me.

I didn't bother switching on Dad's artificial lights. The lick of the orange flames from below the building shone through the window enabling me to see the gate and the keypad.

I've no idea why I got nervous about it as I've snuck out frequently in the past and got back before anyone knew I was missing, but I'd never snuck out to meet a human before, especially a boy.

'Here goes.' I typed in New York on the keypad and waited with bated breath.

Chapter Seven

This time I ended up sitting ass down on a bench in an empty street. Snow had fallen since I was last here, and it was freezing. I've experienced the cold before but not on this scale. And to make matters worse I didn't have a jacket. So here I was in the middle of a grand city in the middle of a snowstorm, in a black strapless dress looking more like a corpse than a Gothic beauty. Which is what I came as for the Halloween party, but as you know, I don't look much different at home.

And now I had to find my way to the university. Oh joy. I wished dad had taken us on more holidays on the Earth plane. I would watch the weather forecasts sometimes fascinated by the different seasons. In fact this is the first time I have ever seen snow. It was beautiful.

Walking down the street lit with streetlights, I was approached by two men wielding a knife. They came out of the dark alley as I passed.

'Hello, darling.'

One of the men couldn't have been older than me by the sound of his voice. It was hard to make out their faces as they were cast in shadow. I was stunned more than afraid.

'Hello to you. Would you mind getting that knife out of my face, thank you very much? I have a party to attend and I'm not in the mood for petty mortals who think they can just get what they want by flashing a bit of steel in the air.'

They began to laugh, and the youngest one brought the blade closer to my neck. I looked down at the blade and up at him. A trick my father taught me when I was three swam into my mind. If I was ever in any danger amongst stupid demons or even mortals for that matter, I was to make my eyes flash red. It may sound ridiculous to you, but it was the sign I was the daughter of the Reaper and that they were now 'marked.' That meant, when they would die, dad would know of their naughty deeds and condemn them straight to the Pits. The Pits were the worse place for any soul to end up. They would relive their crimes as if they were the victim. This would be on constant repeat for eternity.

'What the fuck did you just do?' He yelled; when I saw the knife being flung into the air, and the tall male clench his chest, gasping for air.

What *did* just happen? I wondered. The one who held the knife tumbled over grabbing his leg.

'What the hell are you, lady?' He shouted.

'The Reaper's Daughter.' I smiled. I looked to my left and saw small footprints in the snow. 'Lucinda.' I smirked.

I stepped over the two imbeciles and made my way to the university.

'Thanks, Lucy.' I said.

There was no response as she had come as a soul, but it was a comfort to know she was here and that she was okay.

I had no idea where I was going. As I turned the corner into Times Square, I felt a nudge against my right leg and looked down. I knew Lucy wanted to communicate with me so I pointed to the snow.

'Write something.' I asked.

There was a slight delay which made me nervous, and then, in the snow I saw lines being formed into letters.

'Dad, what?' I said, eager to know.

Dad is in serious trouble.

'Oh no.' I got to my feet clasping my forehead. What do I do now? I hated making big decisions like this. 'Okay, Lucy, let me get to the Halloween Ball, if only for a few minutes, and, if like Cinderella I have to make a run for it, then so be it. But, please give me a few minutes. I really want to see Daniel again. Besides, Uncle Patrick is there. He can sort him out.'

I arrived at the entrance to the university, a little worse for wear. I had the art of 'cutting it fine' down to precision. It was smack bang on nine o'clock. My only concern was, would he remember being a soul, and more importantly, would he remember me and our meeting on the sidewalk?

'Do I look okay?' I whispered to Lucinda. I felt a pinch on my arm, which I took as a yes. So we both waited for a little while in silence. It was when I felt her presence disappear I sensed Daniel.

'Lumiere?' I heard.

My heart did a little leap as I turned to the steps to face Dracula. No, not the real one. It was Daniel.

'You look beautiful.' He gushed.

'And you look quite dashing too.' I replied. 'No Thor?'

'Oh, he's at home with Mum.'

Oh, yes, then I remembered, his dad, the crime lord that is threatening my father. That bit of information may have slipped my mind. But it didn't mean that he was like his dad. And so far no memory of what happened to him.

'Shall we?'

I slipped my arm in his and walked into the ballroom. It resembled my bedroom on a good day. Bats, cobwebs, skeletons, you name it, it was here. It felt as though someone had sprung a surprise party for me.

'Lumiere?' Daniel tapped my shoulder. 'Would you like a glass of wine?'

How could I refuse?

'Yes, thanks.' I took the glass and drank it in one go. He looked bemused and then burst out laughing.

'You're crazy.' He hollered above the music.

'It's my middle name.' I joked, but it was more or less true.

I wasn't the type to stick to rules as we have already established.

The DJ turned the music down, and a gentleman got up on stage holding a microphone. Everyone stopped what they were doing. And as the chatter died down, Daniel leaned into my ear.

'That's my dad, he's the on the board of governors.'

His dad? I felt alarmed.

The man was short, with silver hair and a nice, jolly face. He looked like someone's huggable granddad, not an underground crime lord that is threatening the Reaper.

'Excuse me a moment.' I said and made my way through the throng of the crowd.

I had to get in touch with Lucinda; I heard someone screaming at the end of the corridor.

'There's someone claiming to be the Reaper on television.' The voice shouted.

I soon realised that they weren't screaming in terror but laughter.

'What did you just say?'

The young woman, who was looking down at her phone, lifted her head and called me over.

'Come and see.'

My hopes of it being a random movie I have never heard of were dashed when I saw my dad's face on CNN. Oh my gosh, he had taken over the entire planet's TV stations.

Chapter Eight

Now I started to panic. If Dad was on Earth he was going to be in so much trouble with my grandparents. I haven't spoken about them much, have I? They are the Universe. The Ying and Yang that is life. They set the balance and order to things, and when they are disobeyed they give out punishments. They tend to be as kind as they can to the human race. But where Dad is concerned they go tough on him. I had no idea if they knew of his gambling debts yet but if Uncle David is involved it's more than likely.

'Lumiere. I'd like you to meet my father.'

I stood in the foyer regretting coming here in the first place. I turned around with the biggest fake smile I could manage.

'Sorry, I had to come out for air.' I lied through my teeth.

'Dad, I'd like you to meet, Lumiere. The girl I told you about last night.'

'Lumiere?' He held out his hand. 'That is a rather unusual name.' His eyes seemed to light up and I thought he was taking too much interest.

Reluctantly I shook his hand.

'Yes, it's my mum's favourite French word.' I realised I was giving too much information away. He already seemed to know an awful lot about my family. But did he know of me? If he did, surely he wouldn't recognise me? Shit. This hadn't occurred to me until now.

Daniel seemed to be on edge and I soon found out why. Two men in black cloaks walked into the foyer and stood next to me.

'Who are these?' I asked, jerking a thumb to the one on my left.

Daniel turned away looking guilty.

'Lumiere. The Reaper's daughter?' He exclaimed.

'Leave my dad alone, you hear me?' I screamed. 'And you,' I yelled to Daniel. 'How could you betray me like this?'

'I'm sorry. I was forced to do it.'

'Shut up.' Yelled his father. 'Get him out of here.' He spoke to the one of the hooded idiots next to me.

I did believe that he didn't want to set me up but I wasn't going to give him the satisfaction of knowing.

'You are messing with the wrong people, you know that?'

He laughed.

'You think? Your father shouldn't have borrowed money he couldn't pay back that's what's wrong about this.'

'So what are you going to do, huh?'

'If he can't pay it back, I will hold you ransom until he exposes who he truly is. The world could do with a bit of shaking up if you ask me.' He sniggered.

He was an evil bastard by the looks of it. I thought I knew some creeps in my time at Hell, but this guy was sorely messed in the head if he was going to expose Hell to the human race. Or get Dad to do his dirty work for him. I had to stop him. Both of them.

I swerved around, kicking one of them in the chest and made for the doors when an electrical charge went through me, rooting me to the spot. Oh the bloody pain tore through my muscles and there was nothing I could do right now until it wore off. I allowed them to take me outside and shove me in a black unmarked car. Wherever they were going to take me would lead me to Dad.

Lucinda where are you, girl?

Chapter Nine

According to what I heard sitting in my cell, dad was still talking on the TV stations and they couldn't figure out how to shut him up. I had no idea if he had spoken about Hell yet, because let's face it, if he is admitting to the world who he is, he has to prove it somehow and I think I knew what he'd do. I began to regret my foolish actions as I realised I had been set-up. But by who? Surely Uncle David wouldn't have allowed it to get this far.

I heard footsteps approaching from the hallway, and despite being tied at the hands and legs, I wriggled myself up on the seat and fixed my stare towards the door. I wasn't about to take any shit from them.

There was a muffled conversation going on outside and then I heard the door unlocking, followed by a few latches being slid across. Bloody Hell, what did they think I could do pinned to this chair.

The door creaked open, and I mentally prepared myself for what would come next.

'Lumiere?' I heard a whisper.

I opened my eyes to see Daniel kneeling, untying the rope around my feet. He could've at least untied the gag around my mouth first.

'I'm sorry, Lumi.' He looked up. 'I had to let them take you or dad would've been suspicious.'

He stood up, and untied the gag. I could smell his cologne which I wouldn't forget in a hurry, and caught sight of his chest from the open black shirt he wore. Why did he have to be gorgeous *and* an asshole.

'Why did you do this to me?' I yelled as I got to my feet. He was a little taken aback, and I regretted my outburst.

'Look, Lumi...'

'Oh it's Lumi, now, is it?'

'I had no choice to do what I did, but when I got talking to you, I realised what a beautiful and intelligent girl you were, and dad was an idiot to ask me to do it in the first place.'

'And what did he do? Hang on, mister, how did you know I'd be in New York at exactly the time that I was?'

He turned his head towards the wall. I knew that look, it was guilt.

'Oh come on, tell me. My dad is about to unleash Hell on Earth. Do you really want that to happen?'

'No. I don't. Okay. Your dad and mine were at a poker game one night and your dad... what's his real name by the way?'

'The Reaper, but relations call him Grimm. It's his first name but don't tell him I told you that. Well?'

'Well, the Reaper asks my dad if he could borrow money. He said he was good for it and it would be paid back. Except it wasn't. Dad invited him over one night for a game and during one of your dad's drunken soirees, he told my dad everything, even proved it. I have no idea how he managed that but my dad vowed to expose him if he didn't pay up.'

'So how did you know I was in New York?'

'Your friend, Ulrich. He told my dad everything. Well, dad paid him to tell him everything.'

'That bastard,' I screamed. No wonder he buggered off when we arrived in New York.

'Lumi, we don't have much time. I need to sneak you out of here, come on.'

He took my hand.

'Trust me.' He pleaded.

I looked into his eyes and I felt secure. My instinct has never let me down. 'I do trust you.'

He edged around the door.

'There's nobody here. Come on.' He whispered.

'Where the hell are we, anyway?' I whispered, running up the corridor.

'Dad's house.'

'It's huge.'

'Yes, he can afford it.' He laughed.

We reached the end of the corridor, and Daniel pulled me upstairs.

'Where are we going?'

'The front door is secured, so we'll go to my room and climb down the fire escape.'

'Won't your dad know I'm missing?'

'Not for a while. I've managed to bribe the security at the door.

We got on to the top landing and I could hear his mum in the bathroom, singing.

'Does your mum know about any of this?' I asked.

'No. Get in.' He whispered.

I had never been in a mortal's boy's bedroom before and I was mighty impressed that it was immaculate. He rushed over to his desk and switched on his laptop.

'I need to check what's happening. Fingers crossed your dad hasn't gone nuts yet.' He looked over his shoulder at me. 'I meant that in the nicest way possible,' he smiled. 'Sit down.'

I looked around for a chair but there was nothing. So I flounced on his bed.

'You know, if dad has said anything the entire world would have its dead walking around, don't you. Imagine how overpopulated the cities would be then.'

'Are you kidding?' He swerved around.

'Nope. That's how he'll prove it. We can't let that happen, Daniel. I'm quite fond of this place. Hell is great, and it's my home, but it's all I've ever known. I want to discover new things, experience new places. I can do that here.'

'I'm sure it won't come to that. Anyway, your dad is causing a storm everywhere.'

'Yeah?' I got up to look. And he was right.

On every channel in the world, there he was sat on his throne, in his best leathers yapping away about the best place to buy black shirts. What has got into that crazy mind of his the last few days?

'What are people saying?' I asked.

'I'm scrolling through social media now and people think it's some kind of joke, but the governments across the world are going fucking crazy thinking he's a terrorist.' He laughed.

'The Reaper is a terrorist now?' I laughed too, I couldn't help it.

'So what do we do, Lumi? You know him best.'

'I think the best thing is to get out of here before your dad finds out I'm gone.'

'Good idea.' He opened the French doors to his balcony. The moonlight spilled in and I could feel its energy coursing through me.

'Are you okay?' He asked.

'Yeah. The moonlight gives me energy.'

He didn't seem fazed.

'I don't suppose you'll need help to get down here,' he said quietly, taking rung of the ladder.

'No. I'm quite capable.'

'Of course, I didn't doubt you.'

We ran across the manicured lawn to the back gate when I heard the terrified screams of a woman. I turned and looked up to the window and saw a couple of shadows behind the curtain.

'Mum!' Daniel cried. 'That's her room. Lumi, we have to go up there.'

He was about to make a run for it, but I knew that whatever it was up there had already taken his mother to the Otherside. Of course, I didn't really want to tell him that right now unless I had to.

'No.' I pulled him back. 'Whatever is up there, you don't want to know. Sorry, but there's nothing we can do now.' I yanked the gate open onto an affluent suburban street. 'Where are we?'

'Upstate New York.' He said, choking back the tears.

I realised I wasn't very tactful about his mum, and I felt a twinge of emotions stirring up inside me I hadn't experienced before.

'Look, I'm sorry if I've come across as being a bitch but we must find out what was in your house before anyone else gets hurt.'

'You're right.' He shifted uncomfortably on his feet and took a slow breath. 'Okay, what do you think we should do?'

I glanced up and down the street. So far it is quiet, but I smelled chaos and disaster if I didn't hurry up and do something.

'Aaarrghhh. I can't bloody think at the minute.'

Daniel grabbed my wrists and looked intently into my eyes.

'Lumi, you're the Reaper's girl and pretty damn awesome, if anyone can stop your dad tonight, it's you. Now think.' He pleaded.

'Right. Dad's on the TV talking shit, for now. Let's hope he continues with that. But I feel things have begun to escape from Hell already.'

'Where would they come from?'

'The graveyards.'

Chapter Ten

He would unleash Hell on Earth and you know what that meant. Zombies. I grabbed Daniel's hand and ran up the street.

'We're not going to a graveyard are we?'

'Chicken, are you?' I laughed.

'No. If I was I wouldn't let you drag me up the road in two inches of snow.'

I wasn't prepared for what happened next. We had just crossed the road when out of the shadows came Ulrich holding a red poker in his hand.

'Oh my God, what is that?' Daniel screeched, taking a step behind me.

Ulrich's face was contorted with rage; his dark beady eyes were full of mischief and terror. I wasn't overly concerned about his ugly face but the poker he had is the most lethal thing in this entire universe. It could kill immortals, and if we die, the entire universe would fold in on itself and there would be nothing. Imagine what nothing would be like? It's impossible.

'Where did you get that from, you little scab?'

'I guess your father shouldn't be too trusting, eh?' He sniggered.

He started towards me and raised the poker.

'Daniel, get back, don't let that touch you.'

'What is it? What's he?'

'He's the little snitch that was supposed to be working for my father and that in his hand can turn everything to dust.'

'So that's Ulrich. Was he the thing that hurt my mother?'

'More than likely. So what do you want?' I asked, not really in the mood for bargaining with him.

'I've been promised a much better life on the Earth plane but only if I obliterate you and your family first.'

'Not if I've got anything to do with it.'

I pushed Daniel away, lifted my dress, and aimed a sharp kick into his left side. He stumbled, but the poker remained in his hand.

'Ooh you little bastard.' I yelled, about to stomp my foot down on his face when I saw moving shadows from the top of the road. 'Zombies.' I yelled when Ulrich vanished.

'Where?' Daniel asked, taking hold of my arm.

'They're coming down the street. Let's go. I need to find my dad.'

'Here.' He reached into his trouser pocket and took out his phone. 'He's talking about life in Hell. On the Saturday Night Live Show. Fuck. He's not far from here.'

'Dad is on an actual TV show?'

This was one of his ambitions. I wouldn't have said much if he did it without having to destroy Earth in the process. He only had to say two words, and these words spoken from the Reaper's mouth would have an irreversible effect on everyone. 'Come on. We'd better go before people start noticing the zombies.'

He threw me an incredulous look.

'If they haven't already.'

It was freezing, and the graveyards were waking up one by one. It wouldn't be long until the entire population of Hell would be on Earth. We hailed a cab to Times Square just in time to find Daniels' dad entering the building.

'I don't think he knows I'm missing yet.'

'No, all the better.'

He opened the door in a fit of rage and slammed it closed. I didn't have any money, so I asked the driver if he wouldn't mind waiting whilst I went in the building to see someone.

Thanks to my charm, I got the man on the desk to let us into the studio. I told him we were part of the Halloween act they had booked and we were running late. Another lie, but hey it wasn't like I would be sent to Hell for it.

We crept down the corridor when I felt a tug at my dress.

'Lucinda?' I whispered.

I felt two tugs now and an insistent pull on my dress as though she wanted to lead me somewhere.

I followed her lead when I glanced over my shoulder. Daniel had gone.

'Lucinda, where's Daniel?'

She brought me to a door, and I felt another tug but this time it was very insistent.

I opened the door when I felt a hand clamp around my mouth.

Chapter Eleven

Being tied to a chair twice in one night was grating and to be honest, very unoriginal. A light flickered on, and when my eyes adjusted to the brightness, I saw them all standing around me with their arms folded. Mr. Lee wasn't very happy.

'You must think you were clever to escape, huh?'

It was Daniel's dad, and he was seething. I shrugged.

'He will do it, you know. In less than ten minutes. If he doesn't come up with the money he will tell the world the secrets that have been kept since the start of the universe.' He laughed.

'You can do what you like but the universe knows what's what. All this will come back and kick you in the ass one day.' I said casually.

I was just my usual, cool, calm, cold self. This unnerved him a bit. I could see the flicker in his eyes. He straightened his shoulders. His eyes still bore down on me but they weren't full of the self confidence that I had seen previously.

'We have zombies roaming about the place and the stink of rotten flesh is already shimmering in the air. People, your fellow human beings are going to be freaking out. Do you have family and friends you care about, Mr Lee?' I asked.

'What's it to you?'

'Imagine how scared they're going to be. How could you do this to them?'

He opened his mouth to speak but nothing came out. He seemed to have second thoughts.

'I don't care.' He spat.

The door opened, and a man stuck his head around the door.

'Sir, the Reaper is about to make an announcement. If that's not all, reports are coming in about zombies walking the streets. It's manic out there.'

'Then it's time.' He laughed. 'Come on you lot, let's witness this remarkable event. We'll see to the girl later.'

They left the room and I sat wondering where the hell Daniel had gotten to. I looked up at the clock on the wall. It was almost midnight. I'm not the type to give up, but everything seemed pointless, that was until I heard the door creak open and in walked Daniel.

'Where have you been?' He asked.

'Nowhere. Where have you been?'

'For a few minutes I couldn't see you. You were there one minute, gone the next, so I went to check in some rooms.' He untied me again.

'Thanks. I'll try not to get myself tied up again tonight. It's getting draining.'

He laughed. 'Come on, I found the studio doors.'

'No, wait. Your dad is in there.'

'Oh no.'

'I've thought of something.'

'What?'

'My sister could help.'

'Your sister?'

'It's hard to explain, but she came dressed as a soul for Halloween, so her touch is limited, but she could scare your dad, giving us enough time to get into the studio to stop mine from doing something reckless.'

'Cool. Then ask her.'

'Oh, she has already heard.'

We sneaked out of the room when we heard screams. The door burst open and Mr. Lee and his entourage ran down the corridor to the exit.

'Come on.' I grabbed Daniel's hand and dashed across the hallway. We waded through the crew members stood around the cameras when I saw Dad sat on the couch. The presenter was just about to say something when a member of the audience shrieked. The cameras panned to the woman stood pointing to the doors.

'Now what?' I whispered to Daniel.

I followed his gaze. There was Ulrich on the top step with half a dozen zombies standing behind him.

'Follow my lead.' I said to Daniel as I casually walked on stage. Dad jumped out of the chair and the poor presenter looked on as the zombies followed Ulrich down the steps.

'It's all part of the show, people.' I winked to Dad hoping he would follow my lead.

'He has the Red Poker.'

'I know.'

I hoped the audience would play along too and see it as part of the Halloween theme night but many of them were getting edgy. Ulrich reached the bottom step and ran towards Dad wielding the poker in the air when Daniel ran and kicked it out of his hand.

'No, Daniel. Don't.'

But it was too late, he lay on the floor. Dead.

'Traitor.' Dad yelled at Ulrich. 'I've always suspected you were you getting your nose too deep into my business.'

His anger was flared, and when his anger got to boiling point everybody within a mile of him had better look out. Flames burst from the ground by his feet and his eyes glowed red. The presenter ran off stage and the audience now wrapped in the theatrics applauded. I ran to Daniel and lifted his head, grateful it wasn't me who had to take him now. I looked over my shoulder and Dad had Ulrich by the scruff of the neck. The red poker lay on the ground. I ran to pick it up when Mr. Lee grabbed it.

'I had a feeling you would be up to something.' He sniggered, pointing the poker at Dad. 'Go on, say it.' He yelled at him. 'Tell the world who you really are.'

'No. I will not. Lumi has made me see the error of my ways. Now, give me that poker and we will all leave here intact'

'Not until I have the money you owe.'

'And how much would that be?' Came a familiar voice from the side of the stage.

'Uncle Patrick?' I exclaimed.

'How much?' He asked walking forward.

'Just over a million dollars,' he said.

Uncle Patrick manifested a million pounds in cash on the floor, and the audience gasped.

'Give me the poker and leave.' He said angrily. 'And don't ever mess with Hell again, do you hear me Mr. Lee? Your place in Hell has already been reserved.'

It was only now Mr. Lee noticed his son lying on the floor. He looked at the money and then at his son. I expected him to do the right thing but nope. He took the money and ran. The audience cheered. Uncle Patrick obliterated the zombies and turned to me.

'What do you want me to do with his soul?' He asked. 'I know he was your friend but I must do the right thing.'

'Could you bring him back?' I asked, almost begging.

'Uncle David believes he should go to The Other Room.' He looked over at his body. Two white figures stood around him.

'Please, let him live. He saved my life. He saved everyone's life.'

'But that was his purpose in this life. He has served it now, Lumi, so he should rest before his soul will be returned in another life. In another time.'

'No. Bring him back.' I pleaded, looking over at dad.

'Do as she's asked.' Dad said to Patrick. 'I'll take full responsibility.'

Patrick sighed. He had heard that response from Dad a thousand times before. If wasn't for me, he would not have given into him this time just like he wouldn't have given him the cash. As the Reaper he could not give himself luxuries with his own power

He brushed the Angels away and clicked his fingers. Daniel got up, gasping for air.

'What's happened to me, Lumiere?'

This was the second time he has risen from the dead and he did not even know it.

The presenter took to the stage wiping his sweaty forehead with a tissue, encouraging the audience to give Dad a round of applause, thinking it was all part of an elaborate Halloween act.

Chapter Twelve

So Uncle Patrick saved my dad from exposing himself by loaning him money. And I had gained a new friend. Except that has come with a clause. As Daniel had physically died twice it had upset my grandparents. To set the balance right, Daniel had to be told everything, and he was to become a Reaper's Soul himself. Of course, it was up to me to tell him.

I arranged to meet him at a café the next morning. Dad was gracious and practically ushered me on the Shute. The last thing he wanted was to get into any more trouble.

'See you later, Lumi and please do as you are told this time.' I threw him a mocking glare.

'You are a fine one to talk. I get my adventurous streak from you.'

'What can I say to that? But, hey, I did a good job with you. Proud of you daughter. Now go and get him.' He chuckled and turned to leave the room.

'Here we go, again.' I punched in New York on the keypad and within seconds I was sat in a diner, a little spun out by the ride but for once the machine had got the destination down to precision.

'Can I take your order?' A waitress asked, looking a little perplexed by my sudden appearance.

As I flipped over the menu, the door opened and in walked Daniel. I expected him to have a sullen look about him after last night and losing his mum to the zombies but he was in high spirits.

'It's nice to see you again, Lumi.' He said, taking a seat opposite me.

He was still human, and I had no intention of taking his soul. He was to accompany me on Reaper's business though I suspected there could be more to this than I had been told.

'Likewise, although I wish it were in better circumstances.' He flicked a look up to the waitress. 'Can I get two vanilla milkshakes, thank you.'

Hang on a minute. He seemed so different than the petrified state he was in yesterday.

'What's happened to you overnight?' I asked.

'Lumi if you think dying twice doesn't change you then you ought to question what are you doing as the Reaper's daughter?' He smiled, taking a hold of my hand.

This was terribly confusing.

'Sorry, could you bring me up to speed with this change of personality. I'm not so familiar with humans.'

He smiled and leaned across the table.

'My eyes have been opened to the wonders of life and death. It's a cycle. I see that now, clearer than ever before. I know my mother isn't gone completely and when I come to work for you, I'll get to see her. And as for Dad, well, I guess it'll all catch up with him in the end.'

I was gobsmacked.

'You are taking this, oh, so lightly. I hope it's not a delayed reaction and you'll start freaking out any minute.'

'No, no absolutely not. So when do we leave?' He asked eagerly, which concerned me a bit.

The waitress put the shakes on the table, and I grabbed one, gulping it down. Travelling from Hell was thirsty business even if it only seemed like a split second. I put down the glass and took a napkin, wiping my mouth.

'Well, there's plenty of time. How about we take a walk around New York first?' I asked, zipping up my jacket, glad I had remembered it this time.

'Sure.' He stood up, took my hand led me out the door.

'Oh wait.' I said, feeling my pocket again. It seemed unusually heavy. 'Dracula.' I laughed looking at the first edition copy I had found in the library. Dad must've slipped it in my pocket whilst we were at the table. 'I've got a present for you.' I handed him the book and the look on his face was pure joy.

'How did you get this?' He asked, holding the book as though I had given him a handful of jewels.

'You'll soon find out.' I smiled as we made our way out onto the street.

It was still snowing heavily. Daniel put the book into his rucksack and slung it over his shoulder.

'And where would the beautiful Lumiere would like to go first?' He asked, taking my hand tightly in his.

'I wouldn't mind seeing where they filmed the Ghostbusters.' I laughed.

'Haven't you had enough of ghosts?' He burst out laughing, but our sightseeing tour was soon interrupted.

We had only walked a few yards up the street when there was a gunshot.

'Lumi.' Daniel pointed to a man lying down on the pavement, blood pooling from his body.

'Do you see him?' I asked, looking at his soul standing next to the body.

'Yes. I do.' He whispered.

'Then he's your first customer. Come on, we have work to do.'

Don't miss out!

Visit the website below and you can sign up to receive emails whenever kelly Hambly publishes a new book. There's no charge and no obligation.

https://books2read.com/r/B-A-EOQF-IYGR

BOOKS 2 READ

Connecting independent readers to independent writers.

www.ingramcontent.com/pod-product-compliance
Lightning Source LLC
Chambersburg PA
CBHW031802150726
47989CB00006B/2846